Little Badger's
BIG Adventure

Written by Rhoda Curry

& Illustrated by Alex Clark

"Tell me a story Grandmamma......."

For my wonderful Grandchildren - Eleanor, whose enthusiasm motivated me to start writing, Jacob and Zara who enjoy having stories read to them.

Little Badger had lived all of his young life at Middle Farm. Indeed he was born there in a cosy underground sett, number three in a row of five, bordering Farmer Don's wheat field and under a row of fine sycamore trees. He lived with his Father, Mother, older Sister and two baby Brothers.

His Grandparents, who were quite elderly, lived in a sett very near to the family. They loved their grandchildren very much and took a great interest in all their activities.

Little badger

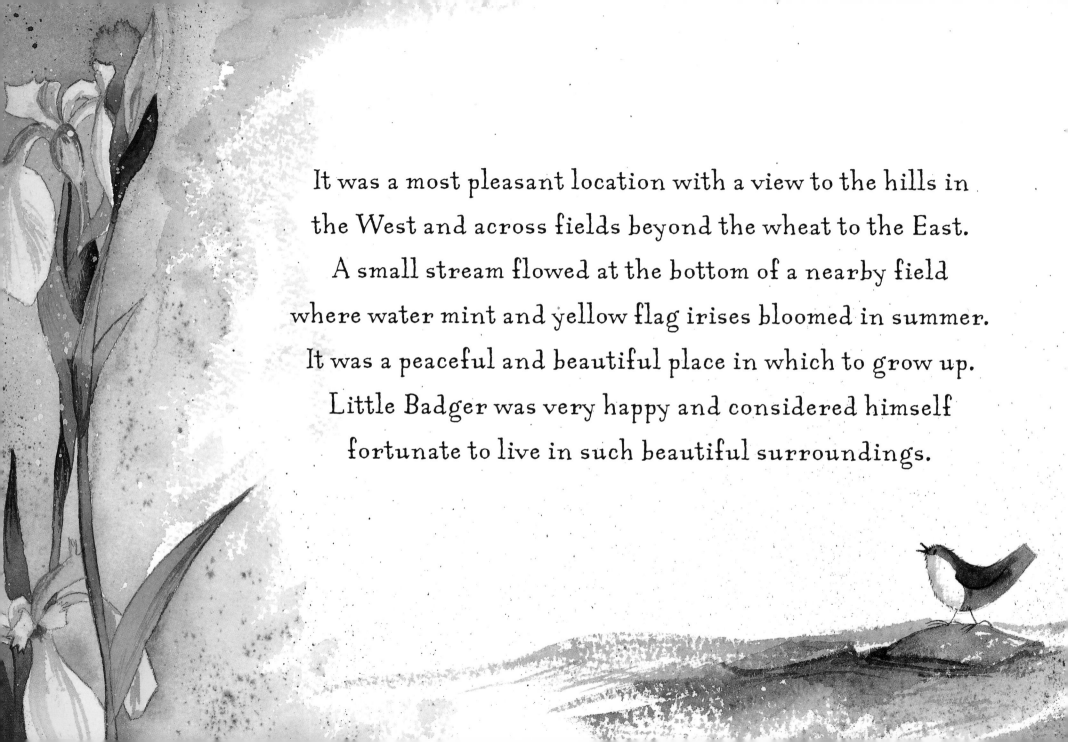

It was a most pleasant location with a view to the hills in the West and across fields beyond the wheat to the East. A small stream flowed at the bottom of a nearby field where water mint and yellow flag irises bloomed in summer. It was a peaceful and beautiful place in which to grow up. Little Badger was very happy and considered himself fortunate to live in such beautiful surroundings.

Generally the badgers had a good relationship with Farmer Don who was a kindly man although he was not too happy when the young badgers played and rolled in the wheat or when they used too much straw to change their bedding. Little Badger had been told how Farmer Don was very cross when his large yellow combine harvester had sunk in the soft earth where Father Badger had extended their burrow to make extra rooms for his growing family. After that, it was decided to confine burrowing to the field border under the trees.

One morning, just before Little Badger was about to go to bed (badgers sleep during the day and go about their work at night) his parents told him that he was now old enough and quite sensible enough to go on his first overnight adventure – of course not too far. Little Badger was so excited he could hardly sleep that day and had to get up several times to pop his head out of the sett to take some deep breaths of air.

worms
wermms
worms, juicy worms

one worm
1

Little Badger was a good natured and well
behaved young badger. He always paid attention
to what the grown ups said. He knew where to
find the tastiest roots and juiciest worms and how
to walk very quietly and keep out of sight.
He wasn't, however, very good at reading or
spelling; but he was excellent at counting.

too
two worms
2

three worms
3
four worms
4

At last, it was time to get up. Little Badger jumped out of bed. He was very excited. He quickly washed his hands and face, remembering to clean his teeth (sometimes he forgot, but Mother Badger always asked) then he dressed with great care. He pulled on dark brown comfortable trousers and hitched them up with his best braces, then a warm fleecy waistcoat with shiny silver buttons. Little Badger preferred to go out with bare feet but he thought that tonight he should wear the thick red socks sent by Nana Badger who was very good at knitting and sewing. He thought for a moment of Nana Badger. She lived far away but visited as often as possible. He would send a letter or perhaps paint a picture to tell her about his first adventure. Finally, he tried on the new hiking boots made especially for this occasion. He hoped they wouldn't squeak when he walked.

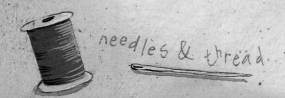

needles & thread

knitting needles

Mother Badger was fussing around making his favourite water mint sandwiches and folding up a clean flannel and a change of socks. Grandma Badger had sent a jar of her special hedgerow berry jam and a small spoon. All of these were neatly packed in his little canvas rucksack. Little Badger who was watching the preparations for the night ahead felt butterflies of excitement in his tummy. He wanted to take his treasure box with him so he popped it in the rucksack on top of the sandwiches along with a small pocket torch which he thought might be useful. Then he quickly fastened the buckles. At the last minute he remembered Toby his small and much loved Teddy Bear. He snuggled him into the warm inside pocket of his waistcoat.

Father and Mother Badger waved goodbye to Little Badger
from the entrance of the sett as he went out into the late
summer evening in the fading light of the setting sun.
He didn't look back. He wanted to appear very brave as he
walked up the hill. He was glad his boots were soft and fitted
so well. They didn't squeak at all. He went quickly at first
then slowed down a little. He wondered where he might go.

Farmer Don's sheep were settling down for the night and
he nodded to two or three rabbits as he passed by.
He did not know the rabbits very well, there were so many of them.
They were always around day and night. Grandma Badger said
they did not have regular mealtimes, or bedtimes.
In fact they were quite unruly and undisciplined.
Some of the little ones were even allowed out in winter
without scarves and so they had constant coughs and colds.

baa
baa
baa

Rabbits

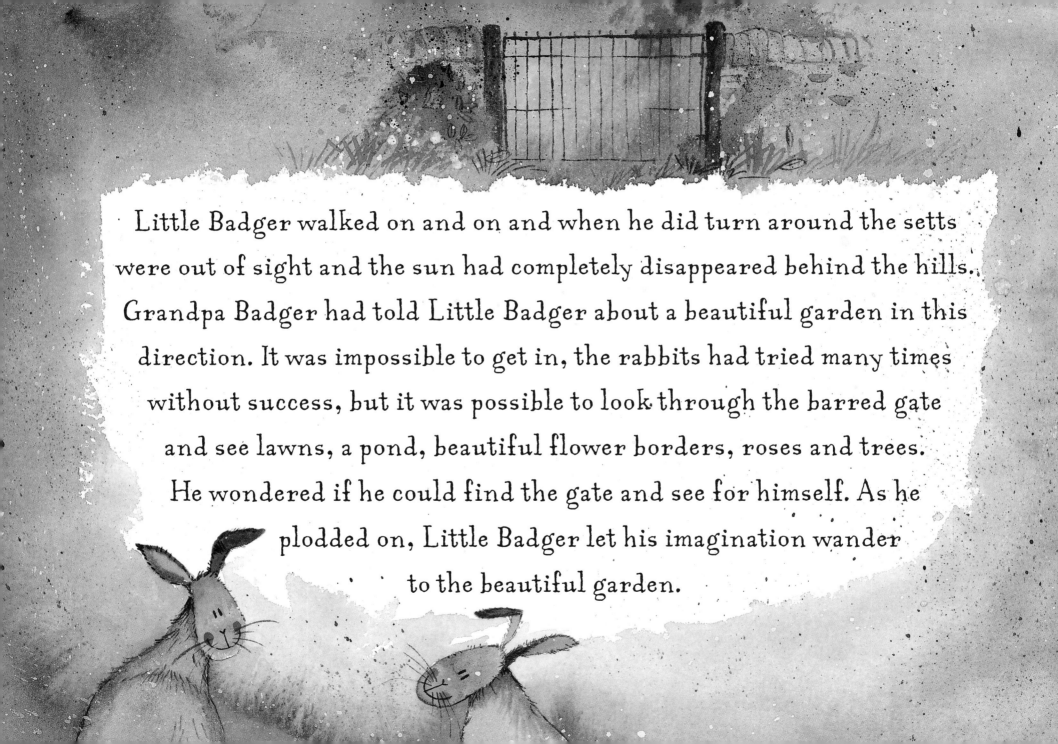

Little Badger walked on and on and when he did turn around the setts were out of sight and the sun had completely disappeared behind the hills. Grandpa Badger had told Little Badger about a beautiful garden in this direction. It was impossible to get in, the rabbits had tried many times without success, but it was possible to look through the barred gate and see lawns, a pond, beautiful flower borders, roses and trees. He wondered if he could find the gate and see for himself. As he plodded on, Little Badger let his imagination wander to the beautiful garden.

He thought of the plentiful supply of worms, roots and grubs that would no doubt be there. He also wanted to see roses. Grandpa knew a great deal about roses — they were his favourite flowers. Little Badger had only seen the wild roses in the hedgerows and thought they were lovely in the summertime, but he longed to see and smell the roses that Grandpa described. Large beautiful and colourful blooms with wonderful scents. He rounded a bend and came on to a narrow gravelled road which he followed, keeping well into the side, almost hidden and safe by the hedge.

woof

woof

Woof

Suddenly a loud bark made him jump. The rucksack shook on his back. Just ahead of him shone a bright light. He saw a huge black dog looking fiercely at him. The enormous dog stopped barking but continued to watch Little Badger whose heart was thumping so loudly he felt sure the dog would hear. He wanted to be brave and almost imagined he saw the dog's tail wag but wasn't sure. "Be brave, be brave," he said to himself, trying to look as tall as possible and taking a few shaky steps nearer. The big dog sat down and yawned as he walked past. Little Badger nodded a greeting, which he hoped the dog would understand.

be brave ... be brave

He broke into a little run, still trembling but very thankful that he was unharmed. He did not stop until he was well out of sight. It was very dark again and Little Badger felt safer with the light of the hazy moon shining now and then as it drifted in and out of the clouds. He slowed down again softly whistling to himself for company. He saw to the left a tiny pathway, no more than a parting in the long grass. He pushed his way through under the trees amongst the willow herb and thorny brambles and suddenly found himself on a small woodland pathway.

Little Badgers

Treasure box

broken china

acorn cups

shiney

white ston

It was very quiet and dark now apart from the evening star twinkling in the sky. The moon had disappeared. Little Badger needed some time to think. He took off his rucksack and sat down. Leaning against the trunk of a larch tree, he opened his treasure box and looked at all his own special things. Some pieces of broken china with a pretty blue pattern, a few acorn cups from last autumn, a small shiny white stone,

clay pipe

soft sheep's wool

pocket handkerchie

L.B.

a pocket handkerchief with L.B. embroidered in the corner, some soft sheep's wool collected from the fields and his favourite clay pipe with a broken stem which he had found when out digging with Grandpa Badger.

He thought of the many wonderful hours he spent with Grandpa, digging or tending the small garden near the stream where Grandpa grew watercress and mint and where he kept his little red boat. Gently, he gathered up his treasures and put them back in the rucksack.

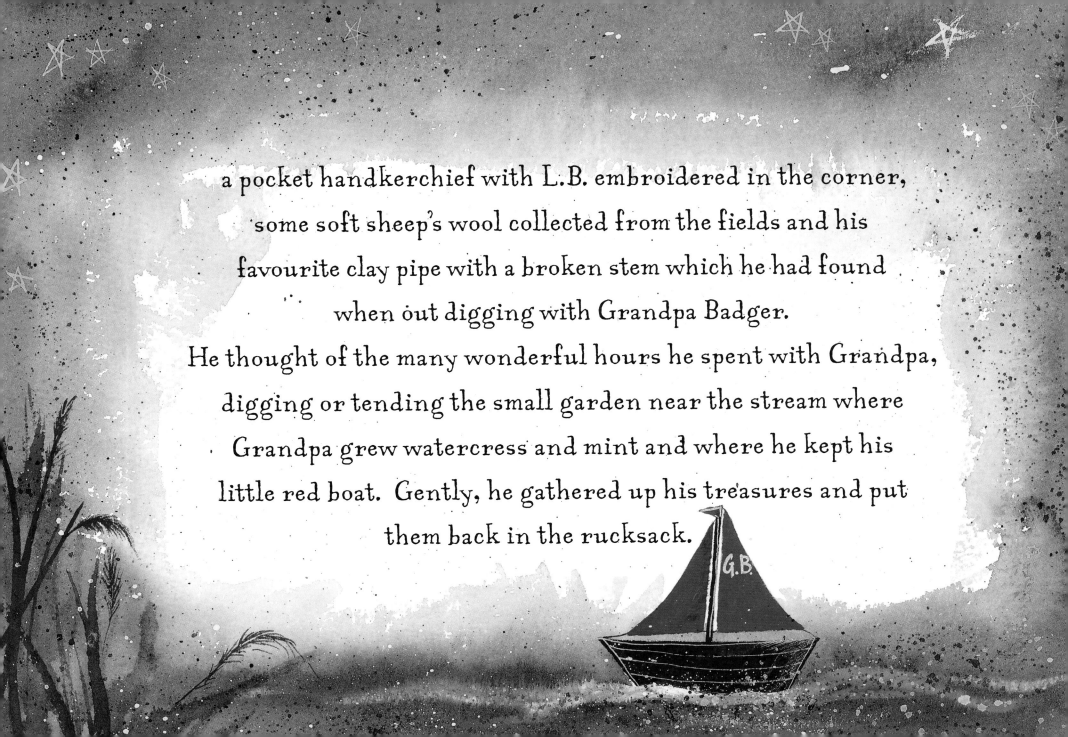

As this was his first adventure on his own, Little Badger was a bit unsure of what to do next. Perhaps this was far enough. He would explore this little woodland and look for the wonderful garden another time. He decided to eat the sandwiches which he knew would be delicious and to have a few spoonfuls of "Grandma's Special Jam". It all tasted so good. After carefully packing up the rucksack, he set off again following the woodland path. He could hear other small animal noises and the flapping of birds in the trees as they settled down to sleep for the night.

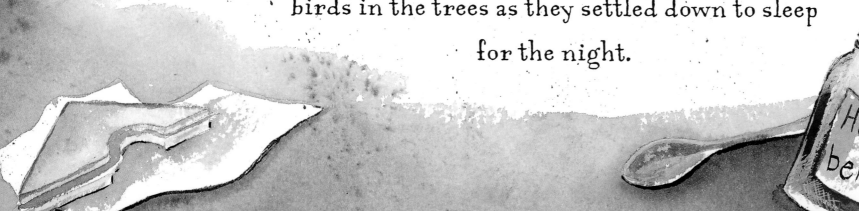

Grandma
Specia
jam

Hedgerow
berry jam

He hoped he might glimpse one of the foxes who regularly passed the setts. No one knew much about them or their families. They led rather secretive and mysterious lives. Farmer Don did not keep any hens, so the foxes tended to go elsewhere for their food. There were many pheasants however. Little Badger was friends with two or three of them even though they could be unnecessarily noisy. They had told him once that foxes were known to enjoy a pheasant supper now and then – particularly for special occasions.
But there were no foxes about tonight.

fox

pheasant

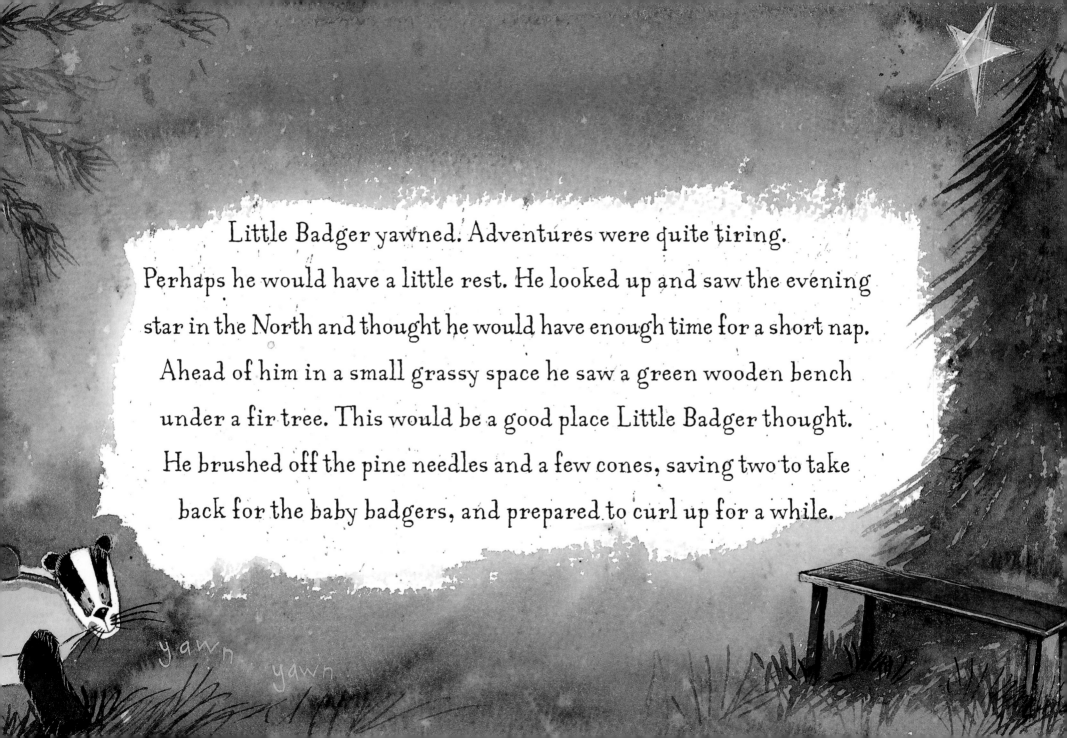

Little Badger yawned. Adventures were quite tiring.
Perhaps he would have a little rest. He looked up and saw the evening
star in the North and thought he would have enough time for a short nap.
Ahead of him in a small grassy space he saw a green wooden bench
under a fir tree. This would be a good place Little Badger thought.
He brushed off the pine needles and a few cones, saving two to take
back for the baby badgers, and prepared to curl up for a while.

yawn yawn

It was too chilly to take off his waistcoat so he just unlaced his boots and placed them upside down beside the bench. Father Badger had told him to do this just in case it rained. He kept the soft red socks on as he was rather fond of them and his feet felt warm and cosy. He could not stop yawning now so lifting the rucksack on to the bench, he lay down and checking that Toby was still safely tucked in his pocket, he closed his eyes and fell asleep.

Little Badger slept for much longer than he intended.
It seemed only minutes later that the sound of early singing
birds and the loud call of a pheasant wakened him up.
For a moment he was so startled that he couldn't remember
where he was. Then the events of the night and his
adventure came to him. He rubbed his eyes and sat up.
It was still quite dark but the dawn was breaking and the
first streaks of daylight were already in the sky.

Little Badger knew it was time to go home.

As he laced up his boots, he looked around. Things looked different in the half light and he wasn't sure which direction to take. Badgers much prefer the dark and would rather not be out in daylight. He started to worry a little. He did not want to spoil his first adventure by getting lost. Mother and Father Badger and his Grandparents would think he was too young to go out alone again if he couldn't find his way home.

squeak

squeak

Oh dear! How he wished it was dark again, and he could retrace his steps out of the wood. Little Badger was just beginning to panic when he heard a soft thud. He had been so busy thinking and worrying that he had not noticed his old friend Sullivan, the farm cat, coming towards him along the path. Sullivan, now sitting on the green bench purring, was a fine ginger cat with a white tip on his tail. Little Badger and Sullivan knew each other well.

Sullivan.

miaow
miaow

Being the farm cat, Sullivan regularly wandered over the
fields and passed by the setts while out hunting. Sullivan was
fond of the badger families. Indeed he was acquainted with most
of the local animals and was afraid of none of them.
Little Badger admired his bravery and was glad they were
friends. It was getting lighter and lighter.

Sullivan, sensing that Little Badger was concerned about this, jumped down from the bench and beckoning Little Badger to follow, set off in a different direction and away from the path. Rough grass, ferns and fallen branches blocked their way. Sullivan easily jumped over them and Little Badger tried very hard to keep up. Eventually they came to a fence which was obviously well known to Sullivan.

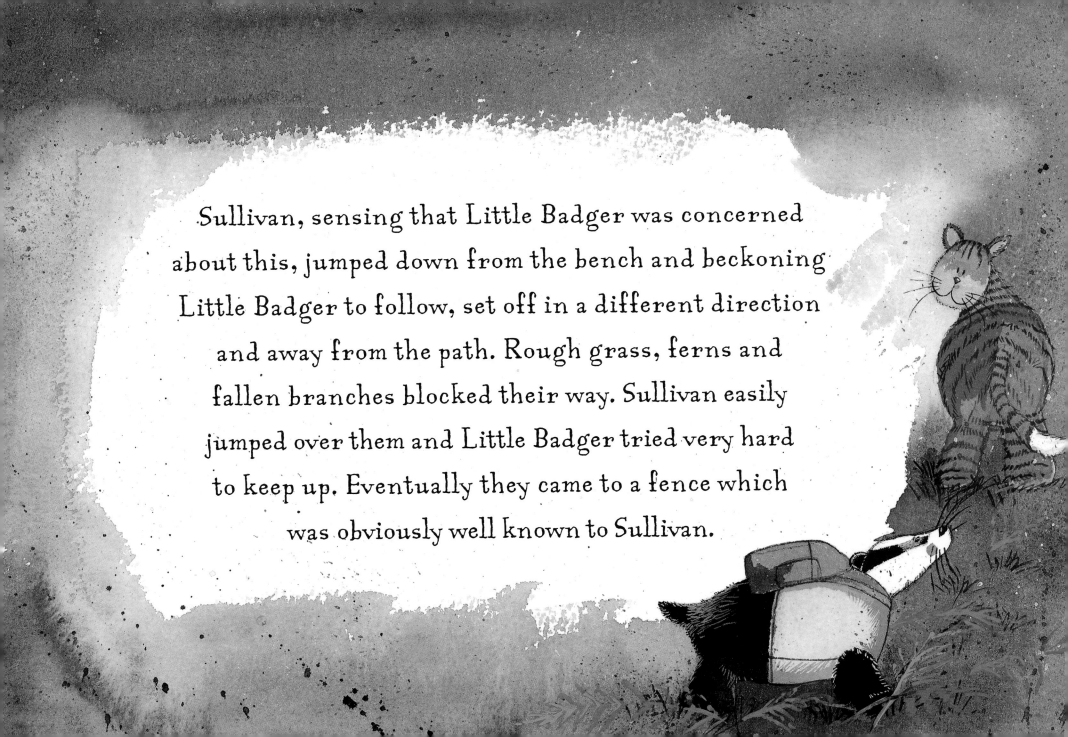

There was a small hole between the wires and the ground and the agile cat crept underneath and into the meadow on the other side. Little Badger found it much more difficult. As carefully as possible, he threw his rucksack over the fence, took off his waistcoat, checking that Toby was still safe. He made himself as flat as he could, wriggled, squeezed and wriggled again until he was through at last.

Sullivan sat close to a stone wall, waiting patiently while his friend smoothed his fur and put on his waistcoat and rucksack again. Little Badger was again filled with admiration for his friend. He thought cats very clever. They knew so many things. The secret ways out of the woods, the best places to hunt and the warmest sunniest spots to doze on summer days. The two animals followed the line of the wall, Little Badger hurrying behind Sullivan who moved quickly and quietly ahead of him. A little further on, some stones had fallen over leaving a gap in the wall. The two animals scrambled over. Suddenly Little Badger saw the field track and recognised the outline of the familiar trees over his home.

Sullivan stopped and let his small friend pass,
watching as Little Badger hurried down the track.
He could now see his Mother who was anxiously watching and
waiting by the door of the sett. Little Badger smiled and looked
towards the trees and beyond to the stream where a blanket of white
morning mist hung over the water in the hollows of the lower fields.
"Mist in the hollows, Fine weather follows" he hummed to himself
as he approached his home. It would be a sunny and warm day but
Little Badger wouldn't see any of it.

"Mist in the hollows
Fine weather follows

He would be fast asleep, tucked up in
his own comfortable bed, perhaps
dreaming of his next adventure.